WALT DISNEY PRODUCTIONS
presents

Copyright © 1975 by Walt Disney Productions. All rights reserved under International and Pan-American Copyright Conventions. Published in the United States by Random House, Inc., New York, and simultaneously in Canada by Random House of Canada Limited, Toronto.
Library of Congress Cataloging in Publication Data
Main entry under title: Walt Disney Productions presents Mickey and the magic cloak. (Disney's wonderful world of reading, #36) A wicked magician gets his deserts when Mickey comes to the rescue of a princess in distress. [1. Fairy tales] I. Disney (Walt) Productions. II. Title: Mickey and the magic cloak. PZ8.W185 [E] 75-23314. ISBN 0-394-82566-7
ISBN 0-394-92566-1 (lib. bdg.)
Manufactured in the United States of America

1 2 3 4 5 6 7 8 9 0   R

B C D E F G H I J K
7 8 9

and the Magic Cloak

BOOK CLUB EDITION

Random House  New York

There once was a merry woodcutter
named Mickey.

He lived in a little hut in the middle
of the forest.

Every morning Mickey took his ax and
went out to chop firewood.

One day, while Mickey was working,
the Old Woman of the Woods
tapped him on the shoulder.

"Do you have any food to spare?"
she asked.

"I have only one piece of bread," said Mickey.
"But I will be glad to share it with you."

"You have a good heart," said the old woman.
"I have been looking for someone like you
to do an important job for me."

Mickey sat down beside the old woman.
"Not far from here, straight down the path,
you will find an old oak tree," she said.
"Seven blackbirds are sitting on a branch,
guarding a fine red cloak. One of the birds
has a bright red feather in its wing.

"Climb the tree and pluck the red feather," she went on. "When you do, all the birds will fly away. Then take the cloak off the branch and bring it to me."

"That sounds easy enough," said Mickey. And off he went.

Mickey walked until he found the oak tree.
Seven blackbirds were sitting on a branch,
just as the old woman had told him.
They looked very fierce.

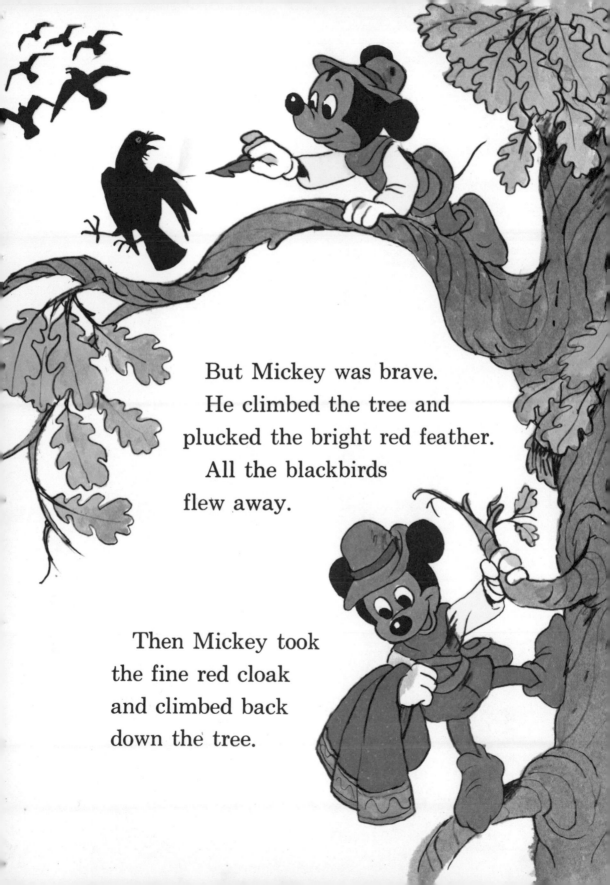

But Mickey was brave.
He climbed the tree and
plucked the bright red feather.
All the blackbirds
flew away.

Then Mickey took
the fine red cloak
and climbed back
down the tree.

Mickey brought the cloak to the woman.
"This is a magic cloak," she said.
"Just put it on and it will take you
anywhere you wish to go."
"Why do I need a magic cloak?"
asked Mickey.

The old woman put it around his shoulders.

"An evil magician has kidnapped Princess Minnie," she said. "He's locked her in a tower because she will not marry him. With the help of this cloak, you can rescue the princess."

Before Mickey could say a word, the woman said,
"Beware! Malgar the Magician is very tricky."
Then she disappeared in a puff of smoke.

Mickey thought he must
be dreaming.
He decided to see if
the cloak really was magic.
He closed his eyes
and wished to be home.

Presto! There he was—standing outside his hut.
"The magic cloak really works!" cried Mickey.
"I guess I will have to rescue the princess."

When Mickey appeared at Malgar's castle,
he saw Princess Minnie in the tower window.

"She is very beautiful," thought Mickey.
"But she looks sad."

He decided to do his best to help her.

Meanwhile, inside the castle, Malgar the Magician was gazing into his crystal ball.

Suddenly he smiled his most wicked smile.

He saw Mickey wearing the red cloak.

"The Old Woman of the Woods gave him that cloak so he could rescue the princess," said Malgar. "But I will get it away from him."

When Mickey knocked at the castle door,
Malgar pretended to be kind.

"May I stay here for the night?" asked Mickey.

"Certainly," said Malgar.

Malgar took Mickey to a room and
ordered a tray of food for him.

"Who is the princess I saw in the tower?"
asked Mickey.

"You must
have been
seeing things,"
said Malgar.
"There is no
princess here."

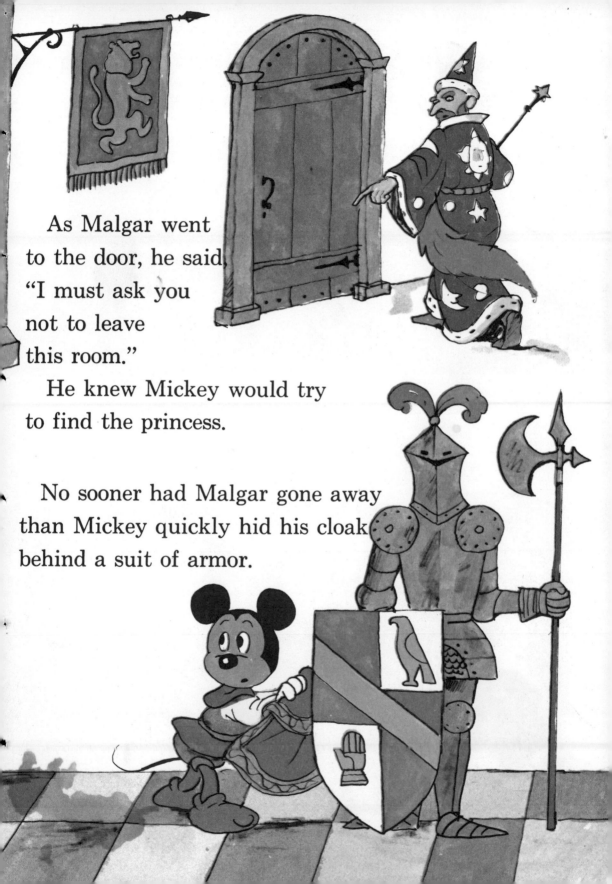

As Malgar went
to the door, he said,
"I must ask you
not to leave
this room."

He knew Mickey would try
to find the princess.

No sooner had Malgar gone away
than Mickey quickly hid his cloak
behind a suit of armor.

Ever so quietly he opened his door
and looked all around.

Then he tiptoed down the hall.

He found a stairway
leading up to the tower
and he began to climb.

Far above him he could hear
the sound of someone crying.

At the top of the stairway
Mickey found a large, locked door.
He peeked in the window.
There was Princess Minnie.

"Please don't cry,"
Mickey whispered.
"I have come
to help you."
"But how can you
get me out of here?"
asked the princess.
"The door is locked."

"Don't worry," Mickey said.
"I have a magic cloak."
And he ran to his room to get it.

When he got there he suddenly felt sleepy.
He didn't know that Malgar had sprinkled
a magic sleeping powder all over his room.
As soon as Mickey fell fast asleep,
Malgar came sneaking in.

He found Mickey's magic cloak
behind the suit of armor.

He took it away, leaving another
red cloak in its place.

When Mickey woke up
he knew it must be very late.
He grabbed the cloak
from its hiding place.

Then he climbed the stairs and gave it to Minnie.
"Hurry!" he cried. "Put it on and wish
to be out here with me."

Princess Minnie put on the cloak
and wished to be outside with Mickey.
But nothing happened.
"Wish harder!" said Mickey.
Minnie wished harder.
But again nothing happened.
"The magic isn't working," said Mickey.

Just then Mickey heard someone
coming up the stairs.

Quickly he climbed
into a large jar
that was standing
outside the door.

He hid there
and listened.

Malgar stormed into Minnie's room.

"Aha!" he cried. "You tried to get away.
But I have taken the *real* magic cloak, so Mickey
cannot rescue you. Will you marry me now?"

"Never!" cried Minnie.

By this time Malgar was furious.
He waved his magic wand at Minnie.
Presto! The princess turned into an ugly toad.
"Ha-ha-ha-ha-ha-ha-ha!" laughed Malgar.
"That's the end of the stubborn princess."

Mickey heard the laughing
and he ran into the room.
"What have you done
to the princess?"
he shouted.

Malgar whirled around and
waved his wand at Mickey.

The next thing Mickey knew
he was in the forest.
"Where in the world am I?"
he thought.

Suddenly the Old Woman of the Woods appeared.

"Malgar tricked me," Mickey explained.

"Don't worry," said the old woman. "We will help Princess Minnie in spite of Malgar's tricks."

The old woman led Mickey to a secret garden.
Two large cabbages were growing there.
One was red and the other was green.
"These are magic cabbages," she said.

She dressed Mickey in a dirty old robe and whispered the secret of the cabbages to him.

"Now close your eyes and pinch your nose, and you will be at the castle door," she said.

When Mickey appeared at the castle door,
Malgar did not know him.

"What do you want, dirty beggar?" he asked.

"I have wonderful
magic cabbages,"
said Mickey.
"If you take a bite
of this red one,
amazing things
will happen to you."

"Bah!" said Malgar. "There is no
such thing as a magic cabbage."
And to prove it, he bit into the red one.

Presto! Malgar became a braying donkey.
"Hee-haw! Hee-haw!" was all he could say.

Mickey rushed past the angry donkey.

He ran up the stairs that led
to the tower.

Then he ran into Minnie's room and gave her
a bit of the green cabbage to eat. Presto...

the ugly toad became a beautiful princess again!

"Oh, my hero!" Minnie cried.

"How can I thank you?"

"Don't thank me," said Mickey.

"Thank the Old Woman of the Woods."

That very day there was a great party for
Mickey and the Old Woman of the Woods.
Princess Minnie gave Mickey a bag of
gold and everyone in the castle cheered.
They were happy to be rid of Malgar.

As for Malgar the tricky Magician—
he spent the rest of his days in the barn.
And he never bothered anyone again.